Zero Sympathy From ME

(Just Sharing)

By (the all-around fantabulous)

Alex M.

Dedicated to Mr. Lovelock: a brilliant teacher.

And especially to Jessica and Julia, who let me borrow their

names.

This one's for you, guys!

September 5

EVERYTHING IS TERRIBLE!!!!

I've been going to middle school for like 1,000,000,000 years now and I just

CAN'T TAKE IT ANYMORE!!!!

But I'm sorry, where are my manners? My name's Jessica, but you can call me

Jess. I'm 13 years old and ALMOST finished with the pit of despair

commonly known as middle school.

me! (Jess!)

Currently I'm an inmate of the 8th grade class of Oakwood Middle School. I've been going there since 6th grade and I completely despised it from the very beginning! I have so many issues with the school that I made up a list of complaints...

My Issues with Oakwood:

- The teachers are major jerk wads

- Too much homework! What am I, a serf in medieval times?!

- The bullies here need to work on their battle strategy, 'cause I can see them coming from a mile away

- The lunch food looks just about as revolting as it tastes

- I require more time at recess and less math class to remain a positive person and not a flaming ball of pure white-hot rage

- Do we really have to have Wellness class? I'm well enough, thank you very much!

- The school is BRAINWASHING US into going along with their silly rules:

  - Everyone has to be "best friends"

  - If you say anything "mean" you get your butt kicked! By the TEACHERS!

  - Everyone has to agree on everything!

  - And why is the school counselor the nastiest woman in school??!!!

Summer just ended and I've been in school for a solid two days now. And let me tell you, I am **completely** wiped out.

Why do people put themselves through this torment all the time?!

What is the point of school anyway?

You go for a few hours, you're bored for most of it, you go home, and then you have to do the very thing you should have been able to finish all that time while you were at school, aka: **HOMEWORK!**

BLAH!!!

Humans aren't meant to sit in a tiny desk for 8 hours a day! We're meant to be frolicking in the wilderness amongst the woodland creatures!

Humans running free
in nature

(And then ultimately being eaten alive by said woodland creatures.)

Humans ultimately being eaten
alive by wild animals in nature

Well actually... the whole *being eaten alive* thing sounds kinda bad. And I bet it's not very fun either.

Yeah, forget that idea!

This week, though, the heat was TERRIBLE! Especially since my lousy school is SO CHEAP and won't pay for air conditioning!

So guess what we get to cool ourselves off with **instead** of AC...

... Rat-Bucket Fans From the 1900's!!!

But whatever. The thing is, my mom bought me this stupid "diary" for my birthday so I could write down my "feelings" and express myself.

(Gross)

My mom is pretty convinced that I need a way to channel my OVER THE TOP energy in a more "proactive" way, so it looks like I'm stuck with this stupid little book until high school.

You see, I have ADHD, so I am, as teachers say, "bouncing off the walls!"

And my mom is **CONSTANTLY** trying to find ways for me to "channel my energy." Usually by performing inane activities, like knitting or arts and crafts.

This time around she's ~~forcing~~ having me try out journalism.

She says it's good for me, but to be honest, the only real reason why I'm writing in this thing is because mom threatened to take away my TV privileges if I don't write about my "feelings."

Normally, I wouldn't care if someone threatened me.

But come on, people! We're talking about the TV here!!!

My daily dose of quality programming is worth a half an hour of me doodling and complaining about junk.

Whatever.

As long as I'm getting free control of the television in exchange for my cooperation, I don't really care.

Me Watching TV

Oh, speaking of my mom, here she comes. She's been pestering me all day to do my math homework.

Yes, I know: I got **MATH HOMEWORK ALREADY!!!!**

It's always something with my mom. One minute she's yelling at me to do math, the next she's screaming about English!

She starts going all, "You need to get good grades, Jessica! It's important for your future!"

And I just say, "Yeah Mom. I totally see how reading a bunch of depressing books is vital for my future!"

And then Mom starts to pout and go on and on about how grades matter so I can get into a good high school and not **DIE** when I move out of the house.

UGH!!!

SUCH A DRAMA QUEEN!!

So on that note, I'm gonna go and pretend to do homework. (At the very least, I gotta try and look like I'm doing *some* school stuff.)

I'll keep you up to date on me some more later!

CIAO! (That's Italian for food, BTW.)

September 6

BRAD!!!! NO!!!

Oh, sorry. I was just playing a video game and this guy named Brad just died a painful, horrible death... **AGAIN!**

It's one of those choice-based narrative games, which in case you don't know, means that the choices I make will decide who lives and dies.

AND EVERY TIME I PLAY IT, **BRAD DIES!!!**

I DON'T WANT BRAD TO DIE!

But I've replayed the game like 13 times now. At this point, I just don't think Brad is meant to live.

But I'm **way** off topic. We're not here to talk about my video game troubles.

We're here to talk about my school day.

BLAH!

Well, it wasn't fun, lemme tell you. But I do have a few good friends who

make things better.

When I was in 3rd through 5th grade, I had this **ridonculously** fun friend

named Alex McGovern, but then I transferred to Oakwood, so I don't get to

see her very much anymore, which stinks. But we do still hang out from time

to time.

Alex Mc Govern

However, I do have some **amazing** friends at Oakwood:

1. My ALL TIME BEST FRIEND EVER, **Will Roberts.** (He's the most FUN

person **EVER!**)

Will Roberts

2. And my second ALL TIME BEST FRIEND EVER, **Maya Ross** (who is the SWEETEST girl you'll ever meet)!

Maya Ross

Those two are the only people who manage to get me through the day. I would probably FLAT OUT **DIE** without them. (Especially since I don't have any other friends.)

I do, however, have quite a few *enemies!*

Well, "few" might be the wrong word to describe the number of my enemies. **ZILLIONS** would probably be a more accurate term.

My mom says that I shouldn't say lots of people "hate" me, so let's just say that MANY, MANY people **REALLY** (very much so) dislike me (a LOT).

But to be frank... they just hate me.

Whenever they come at me, I simply say, "That's fine, you people don't have to like me. I don't wake up every morning to please you."

But SO many people dislike me, for a great variety of reasons!

Reasons Why People Hate Me:

- I'm a slow learner, so class projects are pretty awful for me.

- I get distracted easily, so my teachers are **CONSTANTLY** yelling at me.

- I like to mess with people a lot. (I'm such a prankster! They don't even see it coming!)

- I tend to doodle rude pictures of folks.

- I ditch classes that are stupid, i.e. Spanish.

- I do dangerously stupid junk with Will and Maya in my neighborhood, which most of my neighbors don't like very much.

- CRAZY stuff **ALWAYS** ends up happening to me when I go places.

(Etcetera, etcetera.)

I could go on and on about all my faults, but I'd much rather talk about the cool stuff about me. It's not like anyone is going to do it.

Now as you should already know (unless you skimmed over the beginning of this journal entry), I play video games. But not just play them, **I LIVE THEM!**

I'm one of those people who has a gaming channel on the internet with tips and walkthroughs of all the games I've played. I mostly make videos of more kid-friendly video games ('cause my mom doesn't want me playing "hardcore" games).

I am pretty good at making walkthrough videos, especially since I currently have over 15,200 followers (not to toot my own horn).

Yes I know, it is very impressive!

And yes, you may bask in my glory!

My big dream in life is to get a **SPONSOR** and get PAID to play video games!

I can see it being a good career choice for me.

That is literally my one goal in life!

My dad wants me to get a real job, though. Like being a doctor or a lawyer.

Doctor Jess   Lawyer Jess

EW!

I don't have any interest in that idea **AT ALL!**

Besides, some gaming channels can make a decent amount of money from their videos.

And I read somewhere that in, like, 20 years from now, people who play video games will be in high demand from companies who want them to use their **MAD SKILLS** to fly drones around to blow up gross bee hives or whatever.

Meanwhile, my dad will be in the old people's home by then so there's no way I'm listening to that dude!

ANYWAY.

Moving on from the nerd-fest, I gotta go.

I'm currently writing this in the middle of English class, and I think my teacher is catching on to the fact that I haven't been paying any attention to her this whole time. She's kinda giving me the death stare right now and I just can't afford to get sent to the principal's office for not paying attention in class again.

So I'm out, YO!

September 27

Hey guys.

Sorry I haven't written anything in a while, but I've just been SO **STRESSED AND ANNOYED** lately that I just couldn't even bring myself to write anything!

Now all I would like to say is that: TEAMWORK IS FOR DORKS!

For real.

On my school tennis team (yes my middle school has a tennis team, which should tell you my school is pretty big on sports) EVERYONE IS SUCH A **BUM!**

I just don't understand it.

They don't follow instructions. They don't listen to the coaches. They **whine** about *everything* we do! And they all act like major dumpster-babies!

my tennis team   me

Now I imagine you're saying, "Who cares? It's not your problem."

Well actually, it **is** my problem 'cause I was named captain of the team this year by (the wannabe drill sergeant) Coach Peric, my school's tennis coach slash gym teacher.

Coach Peric

Coach Peric told me that I was chosen to be captain for being such a great tennis player and because I'm so enthusiastic about the sport. And most importantly, I'm perfect for the job! Well, Coach Peric didn't necessarily say that last part, but I know he was thinking it!

I told everyone I knew about being captain. I told my family, my friends, random hobos I found on the street.

Literally EVERYBODY knew about it.

And at first the idea seemed great! I was ready to show off my leading skills, impress the coaches, and go down as the single greatest team captain ever to live!

Unfortunately, that didn't happen.

I found out that my "all inclusive" poop-head school was making me be a co-captain with this REALLY obnoxious girl named Carol!

~~nasty~~ Carol

UGH!

I don't even know why the coaches named her "co-captain" since SHE

NEVER DOES **ANYTHING!!!!!!!**

Well actually that's not true, she does like to talk about me behind my back.

(But she's pretty bad at it since I can always hear her. Seriously, if you're

gonna talk behind someone's back, the trick is usually to do it so that person

can't hear you! Just saying.)

She always says that I'm not fit to be captain cause I'm "*too harsh.*"

I AM NOT TOO HARSH!

I only sprayed the girls with water from a hose ONCE! Like, grow a spine you

big babies, am I right?

The problem is, Carol is a **MAJOR KISS UP!** All the coaches love her and all the girls think she's "super sweet." (But, like... **DUH!** With Carol they don't have to work! OF COURSE THEY'LL TAKE HER SIDE!)

UGH!!!

And you should have heard them complaining about having to carry the waters to the games. The 7th and 8th grade girls have always been making the poor 6th graders carry all the heavy waters and snacks to the games because they're the youngest on the team. But that's not teamwork! That's just mean.

And I remember having to do that when I was in 6th grade, which is why I want to get everyone to share carrying the supplies to the games.

But the only person on the team who openly agrees with me is my bestie, Maya.

Maya ALWAYS takes my side with the tennis situation. She is literally TOO SWEET! (Except when it comes to actually **playing** tennis. That girl is a BEAST with a killer right arm!)

But I swear, sometimes I feel like Carol is **intentionally** trying to separate me from the team so she can leave me to die friendless and alone, stranded on another planet like some sort of space hobo!

Fortunately, I only have about two more weeks of this nightmare and my tennis season is over!

Thank goodness!

However, my season isn't over yet, and trust me it will get rough!

Oh, that totally reminds me of this crazy thing that happened the other day!

So I was rummaging through boxes of my parents' old junk a few days ago and I found this old bullhorn. It's really cool, and the best part of all is you can change the settings on it to adjust your voice.

I swear, it makes you sound SO weird!

My personal favorite setting is the one that makes your voice sound like a

chipmunk that's had WAY too much coffee!

(This Is Basically Me All The Time, But **WHATEVER!**)

The next day I brought the bullhorn to the tennis game along with a squirt

gun filled with ice water.

I flipped the horn to the coffee-addict chipmunk setting and when the girls

wouldn't get moving or started complaining like a bunch of sissy-lips, I simply

sprayed them in the face with my shame-water and started hollering in their

ears with my trusty horn.

Me Displaying My Leadership Qualities

Did it get them to do what I wanted? Yes!

Did I get in trouble for harassing the tennis team? Also yes.

Apparently, spraying girls with freezing cold water from a plastic squirt gun to get them to run is "inhumane," and "against school rules," and yelling in their ears with an ancient bullhorn from the 1970's is "just plain rude." Carol was especially mad and kept complaining to the coaches about how I'm a horrible person, none of the girls like me, and I shouldn't have the job.

She managed to convince all the girls that whenever **I'm** in charge I act like a crazed, sweaty, lunatic who occasionally chases the girls around with rakes to make them move.

HOWEVER!

It did get them off their lazy butts and actually running, so I think my method might be better than Carol's idea where we have to be "sensitive" to everyone, but hey, **what do I know?**

It does, however, look like I'm the evil monster on the team now.

OH WELL! I think I can handle it.

September 28

Hey guys.

So I'd just like to apologize for going completely **banana bread** on you the other day. I was just frustrated and needed to vent!

You see, the problem is EVERYONE is always going on to me about their (**really** boring) problems, but when I start talking about **ME**, they just WALK AWAY!

Honestly, so inconsiderate.

I mean, come on! Look dude! I listened to your dumb butt sore story about your math quiz you didn't study for that's after lunch, so you could stand to listen to me for like three seconds!

I SWEAR!

NO ONE LISTENS TO PEOPLE ANYMORE!

I bet if I ran up to a guy screaming and crying that a deadly asteroid is headed straight for Earth and we're all gonna die in 10 seconds, he would just go, "Cool, cool. That's nice," and then walk away and keep playing on his cell phone!

I really don't see the appeal of cell phones anyway.

Will, Maya, and I never play on our phones! *

(*Reminder: Will and Maya are my best friends! But if you honestly can't remember that information by now then you REALLY haven't been paying attention, have you?)

Will   Maya

You know, I just got my first iPhone **THIS YEAR!**

Up until now I've been using my **DEAD GRANDPA'S** busted-up old flip phone.

I'm serious, I got a hand-me-down flip phone!

my old phone

It's not like my parents can't afford a phone that **isn't** 100 years old and

totally broken. They just don't want me to become a Snapchat obsessed

ZOMBIE like other kids my age.

I'm not even into social media, though (to the utter disbelief of Maya who

practically LIVES on her phone), so I don't think my parents needed to worry

so much.

Plus I never even go on my new smartphone anyway. I only ever use it to play video games, but after I beat all of them and was too cheap to buy others, I couldn't find anything else to use the dang thing for.

Will's not into social media either. He and I both post videos on the internet, but other than that we're clean!

Will and I sometimes like to make short films together at his house and post them online.

Will is LITERALLY **DA BEST** filmmaker EVER!!!

He's made over 200 short films and goof-commercials, and he's even won awards for some of his films, too.

I mean, yeah, they're not crazy impressive awards like the Oscars or anything, but it's still pretty impressive and **very** official.

Basically, my best friend is a TOTAL PRO movie maker and is gonna become the next bigshot in the film industry FOR SURE!

He and I have always gotten along cause we have very similar goals in life:

BECOME SUPER FAMOUS INTERNET STARS, WITH AN

AWESOME SPONSOR, AND RULE THE WORLD AT 18!

Seems simple enough for *me*!

Actually, that reminded me of this **CRAZY** thing that happened to me, Maya

and Will last week.

Okay, so my friends and I all live on the same block (thank you small

neighborhood!), and we have this really **nasty gum-paste-crank-pot** of a

neighbor named **Mr. Gribbins.**

Mr. Gribbins

That dude is CRAZY ancient! We have **no clue** what is holding that old fart together.

Now, look, I'm a nice girl. I'm fair and just. I don't just go irritating someone because they're a crotchety old fossil. I have to have a reason to drive them nuts.

That's why I was so delighted when Mr. Gribbins gave me a reason!

I have this lucky tennis ball that I got signed by this lady named Venus at the US Open, she's a SUPER FAMOUS tennis player BTW!

My Lucky Tennis Ball

It's one of my most prized possessions! (Apart from my game console!)

And last week Maya wanted to play catch in the street around 6:30-ish, and of course she just **HAD** to play with the most precious item I own.

"Why?" You ask, I really don't know. I think Maya just likes to play with **my** stuff so in case something happens to it, it's **my** problem!

And you know what ended up happening to that ball?

Maya's jacked-up **SUPER-STRENGTH** throwing arm (she got from playing so much tennis) rocketed that ball straight over my house and right into Mr. Gribbins' back yard!

MY YARD   **MR. GRIBBINS' YARD**

HOME RUN!!

RIP

⌐ Maya throwing my world away

At first we all just stood there in silence.

What just happened didn't quite register with me for a second.

When I finally realized that **my** ball landed in the yard of the ONLY

neighbor that will NEVER give you back anything that lands on his property,

I COMPLETELY LOST IT!

Me Completely Losing It!

I thought I was going to strangle Maya! I was SO mad I couldn't even speak so I just started blurting out sounds.

I straight up DEMANDED that she go into his yard and get my ball back. I could tell that Maya **REALLY, REALLY** didn't want to do that, and I knew that she was sorry for what happened.

I did understand that it was an accident, but not enough for me to **not** kick

her lousy butt over Mr. Gribbins' fence and get my ball back.

"I don't want to go in there alone," Maya said. "What if Mr. Gribbins catches

me?"

"Well, I'm not going with you," I replied. "You flung the thing into his yard.

Now you're gonna fling it back out!"

"Can't Will come with me?" Maya asked. "He's a tough guy; he could help me

find it."

I could tell that Will HATED that plan. I could even see him shimmying

backwards as Maya was trying to convince him to go with her.

Finally Will caved and agreed to help her.

"Okay, I'll do it," Will agreed. "But I'll only help you if you promise to be my bodyguards at school for the rest of the week! Any time a bully comes after me, **you** throw yourselves in the crossfire. No questions asked. Deal?"

"Fine. deal," I answered.

Will has some problems with bullies at school. He's always getting beaten up and picked on (mostly by the girls— ha, ha!). I'm always willing to help him, but only if I get something in return. And in this case, **that's my ball!**

"Okay, Will. Jess and I will help push you over the fence and then I'll come after," Maya said.

"Wait, why don't you go first?" Will asked. "You threw the ball in there in the first place."

"Because," Maya said sarcastically, "this way you can get a head start on looking for the ball. Besides, a lady needs time to prepare before climbing other people's fences."

"OH MY GOSH!" I yelled, "Will one of you please just go get the ball already!"

"Fine," Will said, as he began to pull himself over the fence.

Maya and I Pushing Will Over the Fence

And as soon as Will jumped over, Maya started pretending to have an arm injury from throwing the ball and **conveniently** couldn't manage to get herself over the fence.

Will grumpily began searching for the ball. After a minute or so he was able to find it!

As he was about to throw the ball back over to me, right on cue, MR. GRIBBINS TURNED ON HIS BACKYARD LIGHTS.

Will started having a **FREAK ATTACK** right then and there!

He began running around in circles like a headless chicken and was almost about to flop on the ground and play dead when I yelled at the doofus to get the HECK back over here!

Will ran to the fence and almost made it over when Mr. Gribbins opened the back door and started screeching this UNGODLY sound! Like a vulture coming after its newly dead prey.

Will flopped right off that fence from surprise and face planted straight into the ground.

Then, he proceeded to run around in circles like a crazed maniac as he saw my nasty neighbor approaching.

Mr. Gribbins had spotted Will! (Though to be honest, it's not all that hard to see how.)

Exhibit A:

I guess since it was **Will** right in the line of fire with Mr. Gribbins slowly

hobbling towards him, and **not** me, I didn't understand the true terror

caused by the 90 year old man, which my friend felt.

But for the **life of me**, I will NEVER understand what Will did next!

In that moment of truth, my friend decided that rather than just climbing

back over the fence like any SENSIBLE person would do, his best course of

action would instead be to chuck the tennis ball right in the elder's face!

Even though he can be a coward sometimes, Will has **excellent** aim. So that's

probably why he had zero problem with smashing our poor neighbor directly

between the eyes and landing the old man's fat butt right back on his porch.

My Poor, Poor Neighbor

Mr. Gribbins was **not** moving.

The sad, old dude didn't know what hit him.

"WILL!!??" I screamed, "What the heck, man?"

"Yeah!" Maya continued, "You might have seriously hurt Mr. Gribbins!"

"NO!" I yelled back at Maya, "I mean, why did he throw my ball away? If that thing is damaged you are in so much trouble, Will!"

But I don't think any of that registered with Will, cause he seemed more concerned with the unconscious 90-year-old man, lying lifeless on the ground like a murder victim.

Will cautiously walked over to him. "I don't think he's breathing!" he yelled.

"YOU **KILLED** HIM!!!????" Maya screamed through the fence. "You can go to jail for that Will! More than that... *I* COULD GO TO JAIL! I could be an accomplice to a crime! That's a punishable offense!"

"Calm down!" I yelled. "Just get the ball, Will! If there's no murder weapon, then they police can't trace our fingerprints!"

"Okay," Will shakily replied, as he slowly reached down to pick up the ball.

Then all of a sudden...

SNATCH!

Like an undead zombie, Mr. Gribbins grabbed Will's arm and moaned like a ghost.

Will shrieked (I have literally never heard a boy's voice go up so high) from surprise, and started flailing his arms around to break free from Mr. Gribbins' grasp!

My half-conscious neighbor moaned one last time and passed out on his back porch, AGAIN!

"He's ALIVE?" Will screamed.

"He's **ALIVE!**" Maya screamed.

"He's seen our faces and might call the cops when he comes to!" I screamed.

"RUN!!!"

And with that Will jumped the fence, or he tried to at least. In his escape attempt, the poor boy got the leg of his pants caught on the fence which resulted in him falling head-first on the ground and losing his trousers all together!

Maya pulled Will's semi-naked body off the ground as we fled the scene, leaving Mr. Gribbins on the ground **alive** and with a big bump on his head.

He never called the cops on us after that, but he certainly didn't like us anymore either.

The old cod did threaten to call the police, but instead he settled for calling my parents and getting me grounded for three weeks, after having to personally apologize to him that is.

And to think, I wasn't even the one who threw the ball at the guy!!! Life is so unfair.

Oh well, live and learn.

If you accidentally shoot a ball into a grumpy neighbor's yard, **don't** send in your friend who has a tendency of knocking people out to go get it.

LIFE LESSONS RIGHT HERE!!!

September 30

BOO!

Okay, so if you hate Wellness class, please raise your hand now. (You best be raising your hand bro!)

I **HATE** Wellness!

It's so dumb!

I just sit there and listen to the hippy I know as my teacher, Mrs. Moran (who everyone calls Mrs. Moron — he! he!), rant on about mental health and stuff that causes stress.

Mrs. Moron

Mrs. Moron says that you should be avoiding things that are "stressful" to your "*ora.*"

Well, I for one find Wellness, as a whole, pretty "stressful" for MY "ora" (whatever that means), so I think I should be **"avoiding"** this **"uncomfortable situation"** at all cost.

Plus, she's always saying that if you don't take this class seriously, then you should just not go.

We all knew that this was an empty threat and she didn't *actually* want us ditching class, but last Friday I decided to take her advice and not go anyway.

AND I GOT IN TROUBLE FOR IT!

Like, c'mon, if you **don't** want the kids ditching your class, **don't tell them NOT TO COME!**

That one seems like it should be pretty simple to figure out. But HEY, what do I know?

To be honest, I much preferred gym class to Wellness. At least in gym I got to tackle people and kick things in my peers' faces! In Wellness the most excitement I get is when my teacher accidentally trips over the carpet.

You see, in 8th grade, instead of having gym, we get to have WELLNESS the entire year!

UGH!!!

Okay, so now I know about mental illnesses. BIG WHOOP! How about the school teaches me something I actually might need to know in my life to, you know, SURVIVE!

I wish we had Home Ec class at my school instead. Sure, maybe I won't know the "horrible suffering people with eating disorders have to go through," but at least I'll know how to wash my socks!

Person With Adequate
Life Skills

Person Who Got An
A+ In Wellness Class

There's this real "Mr. Smarty Pants" in my class, too. His name's Dave, and he likes to pretend he's the teacher in literally EVERY SINGLE **CLASS**!

Dave

Sometimes the teachers even let him take over the class because he knows more information on the topic than they do.

He's sort of a nice guy, but as a whole, pretty annoying!

The one teacher who isn't a fan of his "Smart-Alec-ness" is Mrs. Moron. She always starts talking over Dave and saying he's wrong while he's showing off.

I suppose I get where my teacher's coming from. No one likes to be undermined, especially by a kid two DECADES younger than you!

The problem is, I've often looked up what Dave says, and he's usually factually correct.

What can I say, the kid knows stuff.

Still, Dave does like to be snarky and bug basically everyone in the class with his rand-o facts that nobody cares about.

Usually, Will and I just sit in class together passing notes, but we can't do that anymore after what happened yesterday.

These are the notes that we were passing:

Can you believe Dave today?
He's worse than EVER!
What is that guy's deal?
Does he get pleasure from irritating everybody or something?
—Will

I know!
Would he just SHUT UP already!
—Jess

That guy is going to get beaten up SO MUCH in high school!
I've heard kids like him get eaten ALIVE!
Too soft and sensitive.
I almost want to go to the same high school as him so I can see that!

—Will

Me too!
The Poor sod.
—Jess

I bet on the first day of high school he'll end up eating his lunch in the janitor's closet to hide from bullies!
—Will

HA!
That's So mean!
But, like, 100% true!
—Jess

73

Then, all of a sudden...

SNATCH!!!

Mrs. Moron caught me passing Will the paper with our ~~rude~~ notes on it.

So the woman marched herself right over to us, grabbed the paper out of Will's hands, and dragged us to the front of the classroom.

Then Mrs. Moron started reading our notes in front of the class, which was only **EXTREMELY EMBARRASSING!!!**

And I guess what we wrote must have been pretty hurtful, cause Dave actually started **CRYING** right in the middle of the Wellness class!

To be honest, I didn't think we wrote anything *THAT* bad, but clearly Dave felt otherwise. (What a sensitive-sally.)

I do feel mildly sorry for Dave. It's certainly quite sad when a 13 year old boy bursts into tears in public because someone found his incessant talking annoying.

Will is completely right about how Dave's not gonna do well in high school, though. However, Mrs. Moron didn't quite see it the same way.

My fart-nugget teacher insisted that our note was "highly offensive" and "extremely disrespectful to our classmate." But my only comment to that is, if she really thought our note was "*SO BAD*" then why did she read it to the entire class?

I MEAN, COME ON!

If the woman really wanted to maintain the tranquility in her class, wouldn't she just get rid of the paper? I mean, that's what I would do if I were her!

But it gets WORSE!

After destroying the self-esteem of one young teenage boy, she then held us back from going to lunch so we could "*reconnect*" with each other by making **friendship bracelets!**

I don't even make friendship bracelets for people I'm actually FRIENDS with, so **why in the world** would I want to make one for some kid I don't even like?!!

And I don't think that Dave and Will liked that idea either, but Mrs. Moron was pretty stuck on her little "bonding technique."

So my teacher whipped out her balls of yarn and for **thirty minutes** we were forced to sit on the floor and knit hideous bracelets!

Mine didn't look that bad:

Meanwhile, Will's looked like a yarn bomb went off on his hands:

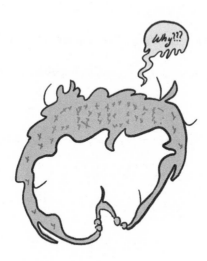

And it's just a guess, but I think Dave was still pretty mad at us from the note cause his friendship bracelet didn't exactly give off a warm and loving vibe:

Now for the rest of the year, we all have to wear these dumb bracelets to Wellness class to keep Mrs. Moron from bugging us about friendship again.

Despite the fact that I do feel mildly sorry for Dave and how sensitive he is, I have a feeling he won't get very far in life.

Let's face it people, the kid peaked in 8th grade, now it's all downhill from here!

Things will get harder for him and in 20 years poor Dave will be cleaning the toilets at Chick-fil-A. Or better yet, WORKING FOR ME!

I do love having servants to boss around!

Anyhoo! I gotta pop off!

I've got music class next, and that's my ALL TIME FAVORITE CLASS EVER!

Literally **NOTHING** could ruin music class for me!

SOMETHING LITERALLY RUINED MUSIC CLASS FOR ME!

And that something is a 120-pound ball of snooty fury.

Okay, so you remember Carol, the annoying butt-clown 7th grader from my school's tennis team, who complained about my coaching brilliance ALL THE TIME!

Yeah, well...

SHE GOT TRANSFERRED TO MY MUSIC CLASS FOR THE REST OF THE YEAR!

The only class at my school that I can stand and Carol just **smashed** it to tiny bits and farted on its remains!

Now, you're probably asking: "Why is a 7th grader in your music class? You're an 8th grader after all."

Excellent question! It's because life is a cruel, cruel mistress, and the universe sent Carol here from the bowels of the underworld to eternally mock my very existence.

That, and 'cause my school likes to merge all the grades together in classes like music or art, so that we may all act like more of a "community."

BLAH!

Community my foot! (Which I **will** be using to kick Carol with.)

I liked music class, because I liked to sing. I was the best singer in the class, and everyone knew it!

Now **Carol** comes along, and with a name that actually has the word "carol" in it, I DON'T STAND A CHANCE!

She's fantastic!

The girl can sing like a GODDESS! Meanwhile my voice is the equivalent of a (drop-dead-gorgeous) angel, **BUT EVERYONE STILL LIKES *HER* BETTER!**

UGH!!!

So now music class is **dead** to me and I am **SUPER** mad right now!

Maya's in my music class too, and when we saw that Carol was joining us, we both just stared at her in horror.

"Why is she coming into our class now?" Maya asked. "It's the middle of the year! Plus she's one of the meanest girls in school."

And for the life of me I couldn't answer Maya!

Heaven knows why Carol's being transferred so late in the year. But at my school, something pretty big has to happen to get you moved to another class at this point. (Maybe she was just *too* annoying for her old class!)

My teacher, (the EXTREMELY DULL and somewhat awkward) Mr. Jarvis, briefly introduced himself to Carol when class started.

Mr. Jarvis

Mr. Jarvis decided to take the formal route when greeting his new pupil, and

went to give Carol a respectful handshake. But the girl just stared at Mr.

Jarvis like he ate her pet goldfish or something.

I guess Carol isn't used to someone wanting to politely shake her hand like

they did in the olden days when people whittled stuff out of wood (or

whatever my parents did when they were kids).

So needless to say, **THAT** handshake wasn't exactly enjoyable for Carol.

Immediately after the hello's and how-do-you-do's, Mr. Jarvis asked Carol to sing for him so he would know if she was a soprano or alto (you know, the pitchy-squeaky singers or the deep manly-voiced singers).

Everyone in class is organized based on what type of singer they are.

The boys are **always** baritones (the deepest singing voice). Even if a boy sings higher than the squeakiest girl in the class (that's Maya BTW), he's still made a baritone.

Mr. Jarvis just likes to have all the boys grouped together, which is **FINE BY ME!**

Keep those disgusting snot-nosed creatures away from me, and you're guaranteed to be my favorite teacher.

Seriously, they are SO weird!

Besides Will (who isn't in my music class), **EVERY** single boy at my school is

the absolute **WORST!**

Why The Boys Are Awful:

- They're GROSS!

- They're obnoxiously rude.

- They make dumber jokes than I do, which automatically makes them a #1 threat to me!

- They're just really stupid (it's almost sad).

No More Explanation Required!

The only plus side to the boys is that they **always** disrupt class, meaning that I get out of having to pay attention. (He, he!)

But the boys weren't my main concern at that moment.

As soon as Carol started singing, Maya began whispering to me: "Wow. Oh my goodness. She's really good!" But Maya immediately stopped speaking after I snarled.

At the same time, the rest of the class was basking in Carol's glory.

Meanwhile, I was barfing in my mouth.

When she finished singing, the class ACTUALLY STARTED **APPLAUDING**

HER!

UGH!

And Carol just did this little "yeah, I know I'm amazing" curtsy and skipped back to her seat while giving me and Maya the death stare, the equivalent of saying, "Eat my farts, skunk-bags!!"

At that moment it dawned on me that Carol was transferred to my music class because she was just too *GOOD* for her old one.

So with the spirit of fury still festering within my dark, bitter soul, I did the only sensible and responsible thing that there was to do: I stuck a piece of half-chewed gum on her chair before she sat down.

Exhibit A:

I was feeling pretty good about myself at that moment, especially when the class was over and Carol stood up to find her fancy (60 inches too short) lady-skirt completely ruined.

The girl almost had an aneurysm!

She started screaming right in front of Mr. Jarvis, but he was such an awkward-sausage that he just started stammering and sent her to the principal's office.

Carol Being A Drama Queen

An hour later I saw Carol walking around in the hallway wearing her gym shorts (nerdy 7th graders like her have to take gym, BTW). It was especially funny since she had a 200 dollar designer shirt on, and was wearing GYM SHORTS with it!

HA!

She did NOT look happy.

And as she stomped past me and Maya, I heard her whisper under her breath, "I'm gonna get you for this, Jess."

That's when Maya started to panic.

I know Carol knows I did it, but *I'm* not all that concerned. What's the worst she could do anyway?

At least the chewing gum scandal made my miserable music class a bit better, for that moment. Cause I can tell you this, it's definitely gonna stink for the rest of the year!

October 3

I HATE CLASS PROJECTS!

ICK!

They are SO lame!

People always say, "If you want something done right, do it yourself." But schools are kinda contradicting that idea by forcing kids to work together.

I mean, I get it!

Kids need to learn how to work with other people, but since I'll most likely be all these losers' boss one day, I really don't think any of this stuff applies to me.

Besides, I do well on school stuff all on my own. Especially on fun artsy projects that I actually care about doing! Those projects mean I actually get to be creative, and funny, and COOL! Then a group project comes along and RUINS IT!

Everyone at my school is a bunch of stick-in-the-mud, fuddy-duddies, who never want to have fun!

But the **biggest JERK of all** (maybe even more so than CAROL) is this obnoxious girl I got partnered with for my latest science class project, Brenda!

Brenda

Even her name sounds obnoxious!

BRENDA!!!

(Duh! Duh! Duh!)

GROSS!

Now my science project, given to us by (my sparkly and EXTREMELY sweet science teacher) **Mrs. Quackenbush** (YES! That's her name!), would probably have been pretty fun if I could do it alone!

Mrs. Quackenbush

Our job was to make a video explaining what makes certain foods healthy and why you should eat them, or whatever, and I wanted to make it funny and interesting, filled with lots of gags on top of the dumb science stuff to make it, you know... **good**.

My Assignment Mrs. Quackenbush Gave Me:

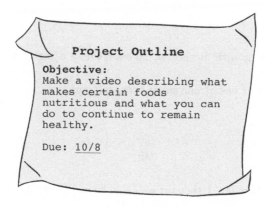

Project Outline

Objective:
Make a video describing what makes certain foods nutritious and what you can do to continue to remain healthy.

Due: 10/8

'Cause, come on! Let's face it people, would **you** watch a video about eating asparagus if it wasn't comical? Yeah, didn't think so.

BUT **NO!**

Every idea I came up with, Brenda would always have a snarky comeback.
Here's an example of one of our **many** conversations:

ME:

Hey Brenda-the-blender, I thought we could have a scene in our video where

I explain how if you eat too much food you'll gain so much weight that you

can't get your fat butt off the couch and you'll DIE! And then we could put in

a picture a fat guy exploding or something!

BRENDA:

Jess. That idea is horrible! We can't do something that ridiculous!

ME:

Okay, well what's **YOUR** idea?

BRENDA:

Oh... I don't have one. But I know that it won't be as stupid as yours.

(The charming Brenda, everybody!)

ME:

So you don't have any ideas, and you're turning down mine anyway?

BRENDA:

Yeah... well, your idea is too *INSENSITIVE* to obese people. And I just

don't feel *comfortable* doing something like that.

(Seriously, I hate that girl SO MUCH!!!)

And I could see Mrs. Quackenbush in the background NODDING HER HEAD

IN APPROVAL AT BRENDA'S COMMENT!!!!

Typical, the teacher will take the evil (and SUPER boring) student's side.

UGH!!!

Our little debate went on like that for about twenty minutes.

Time that could have been spent **WORKING** on the dumb project.

But NO!!!

Every single idea I thought of, even the most boring ones, Brenda had a problem with!

And Mrs. Quackenbush wasn't much help either. The woman just stood next to us, casually nodding her head in agreement every time Brenda shot me down. (Great job teaching us about **teamwork**, Madam-Teacher-Lady.)

And all of that got me to start thinking that maybe Brenda's problem wasn't **MY IDEAS**, it was her wanting to make **ME** look bad!

Think about it, people!

Brenda wouldn't care if I was being "*insensitive*" to anyone, especially not the fat! Heck, if insensitivity was a color, THAT GIRL WOULD PAINT IT ALL OVER HER HOUSE!!!

I bet she just wants to make me get agitated and make a scene in front of Mrs. Quackenbush, so that way Brenda will look like the LITTLE ANGEL and I'll get in trouble again!!!

(Or I could just be paranoid, and am taking this class project way too seriously. Nevertheless, I'm committed to my feud with Brenda now, so no turning back!)

Besides, Brenda never liked me anyway, mostly 'cause I tell her off when she was being a garbage-panda. But that girl is such a major bully that she had it coming!

She's rude to me, to Maya, and literally every single kid in this school! (Teachers *CONVENIENTLY* never notice when she's picking on anyone!)

But sweet Will has it the hardest with Brenda. That girl has been making fun of him and beating him senseless since the **4th GRADE!!!**

For the life of me, I don't understand why she's *SO* stuck on taunting Will above all others. He never even DID ANYTHING to Brenda! In fact, before she started bullying him, Will was nothing but nice to that girl! I even think that at one point they were ***FRIENDS!!!***

Girls are so weird, man.

Plus, I bet that Brenda is one of those kids who have never been told "**NO**" before. She seems like the type who always gets her way, and acts like a BUTT when someone challenges her. And I just so happen to be that person challenging her.

But don't you flatter yourself, Brenda. I challenge everybody! (You're not that special.)

I still think my idea is a knock-out, though. I even made up a rough sketch of it for the video and everything.

What Happens To Fat People:

By: Jessica Yermack and Brenda

(I don't know her last name)

Part 1:

Part 2:

THE END.

HOWEVER! Brenda didn't like my sketch either **because**...

...it was **STUPID!!!**

And at that point I just lost it and was like, "Stupid? It's **true!** Some fat people **can't** get off the couch and **do** die. Sure, maybe they don't **EXPLODE,** but the rest still remains true."

But hey why give all the information, it's only *science class* after all!

I spoke to Will and he completely agrees with me that a film needs to grab your attention and entertain your audience (even if it is for a class project).

The problem was that Brenda just wouldn't cave for any of my ideas!

In the end I decided to change the WHOLE script to make it more to her liking, after she did **nothing** to compromise with me.

Then when we went to go film it I was all ready to dress up and do all the acting (like the movie star I am).

Jess The Movie Star

Then, **Brenda** decided that she wanted other people to do the acting instead of me. So when I wasn't looking the she-beast snuck off and found (you got it) **CAROL!!!!**

NOOOOOOOO!!!!

That was the sound of me internally screaming.

By this point in the year, I've decided that Carol is my worst enemy.

What I didn't know was that **Brenda** was **friends** with her!!! (Though in hindsight, that makes sense.)

The Evil Best Friends

And because of this little "team up," I was catching sass (and bad

acting/directing skills) from all angles!

So I didn't get to do **my** script or **my** acting, and guess what I also didn't get

to do: THE EDITING!

Now as a YouTuber, **I know how to edit!** So I was hoping that I would at

least get to do that.

Nada!

Brenda also went behind my back and did that!

So I pretty much did **nothing** on this project! (And to think, for once I

WANTED to do something!)

And my teacher actually yelled at **me** for not being able to compromise with

my partner! In addition to that, she even took points off MY grade for

Brenda being a sneaky barf-face.

Yeah! I'm serious.

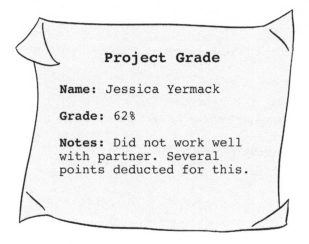

Project Grade

Name: Jessica Yermack

Grade: 62%

Notes: Did not work well
with partner. Several
points deducted for this.

And in response to this insanity, I respectfully turned to Mrs. Quackenbush

and said, "**REALLY?!!** I'm the one who has the issue here? Why isn't that

nut-job being yelled at for not cooperating?"

But I don't think Mrs. Quackenbush liked that question very much since my parents were later sent an email that, in great detail, described my "disciplinary problems" in class.

So now I'm grounded for a week.

Yeah... I am **SO** done with partnership!

Hopefully I get a good partner for the next project I have, but with my school, I seriously doubt it!

October 10

Okay, you will **NEVER** believe what happened earlier today!

It's like something out of a pre-teens book! (One that's probably amazing but will never end up getting professionally published.)

So I was walking down the hall this morning, when I saw the janitor fixing the water fountain. I don't know his name.

(What? How many of **you** know the names of the janitors at **your** school?)

That fountain has been on the fritz for weeks now. I don't know how many times I've walked by and seen people get sprayed.

My School's NASTY Water Fountain

I walked over to the janitor and asked him if the water fountain was fixed.

I don't think he understood me, or he was just rude, 'cause the guy just rolled his eyes and walked away.

To be honest, I didn't really care all that much, so I just let it be.

Later, in between periods, I was walking to class with Will and Maya when Will stopped at the water fountain and said he needed a drink.

But when Will reached down to take a sip of water, the water fountain shot a blast of liquid freshness right over his head and straight at me and Maya. (Nice job "fixing" the fountain, Mr. Janitor-man.)

We dived out of the way like a heat-seeking missile was coming for us, allowing the blast to slam smack-bang into **Brenda!** (My annoying partner in science class.)

The water pressure must have been REALLY strong (or Brenda just wasn't expecting to be flushed away by a blast of water today), 'cause when she got hit, the girl went flying back into the wall, knocking a bunch of kids off balance. They fell like dominoes!

After that moment... **BRENDA WAS MAD!**

The girl picked her soggy butt off the floor and furiously marched over to Will. The look of pure evil was definitely on that girl's face.*

(*Reminder: as I've mentioned earlier, Will gets beat up by the girls at my school a LOT! Brenda is one of those girls.)

Before Will could even open his mouth to apologize, Brenda slammed the poor boy against the wall like she was about to strangle him!

"ARE YOU KIDDING ME?!!" Brenda screamed, "I'm SOAKING WET!"

"I-I'm sorry," Will pleaded, "I was just getting a drink of water—"

"And throwing water on me is part of how you 'get a drink,' huh?"

"Hey," Maya interrupted, "he said he was sorry. It was an accident, so leave him alone."

"AW!!! MAYA THAT IS SO SWEET!!!" I thought to myself.

What? Maya was kicking butt (at least her version of it anyway) over there all on her own. I didn't need to butt in just yet. (Plus, I already get in enough trouble on my own.)

"Oh, what," Brenda said, still holding onto Will, "you need your girlfriend to look after you?"

"She's not my girlfriend!" Will yelled.

That's when I decided it was time to intervene.

"Okay, Brenda," I said, "that's enough. Let Will go."

Then I decided to pull out my **evil eye** stare and go all "OH I DO NOT THINK SO BUDDY" on her butt!

And with that, Brenda reluctantly let go and backed off from Will.

"Whatever," Brenda said as she began sashaying away down the hall. "You losers aren't worth my time."

Once the witch was at a safe distance, Maya asked Will, "Are you okay?"

"I'm fine," Will said as he walked away.

I suppose he must have been embarrassed. Who wouldn't be after getting pinned down and humiliated by some nasty girl?

"Did I say something wrong?" Maya asked.

"Nah, he's just bummed out," I replied. "Give him a day or two and he'll be fine. You'll see."

Then out of the corner of my eye, I saw it.

The one, the only, the monster... **CAROL!!!**

"OOOOO! Hold up!" I said.

I began to track Carol's movements in the hallway. Carefully, ever so carefully. I locked onto my target like a sniper.

Carol took a few steps closer.

"That's it," I said. "Stay on target, stay on target."

BOOM!

And with that I pushed the button on the water fountain and smacked Carol right in the nose with water!

AAAAHHHHHHHHH!!!!!

(That's the sound of Carol screaming her head off in the hallway.)

All I gotta say is whatever that janitor did to the water fountain he sure did a good job, 'cause that thing has some good accuracy on it now. I bet I could bring down an elephant from 100 meters away!

"Wow, that water fountain is **really** broken," Maya said.

"Yeah, well that's what happens when you get some nimrod to fix it," I replied.

However, I couldn't be more pleased with what this magical water provider has done for me! Just think of the possibilities! I could drench every kid in school with this thing! I'd be like a **WIZARD!**

Unfortunately, the dream died pretty fast.

After the 15th person at school got hit with a tsunami, the principal finally had the janitor fix the water fountain... again.

This time it **actually** got fixed.

LAME!

October 13

YESTERDAY WAS THE BEST DAY EVER!!!!

It all started when I woke up to the sound of my mom screaming in my ear,

"GET YOUR LAZY BUTT OUT OF BED RIGHT NOW YOUNG

LADY! You're going to be late for school!"

What?

That's how my mom wakes me up every morning. If she's not screaming at me

then **I ain't waking up!**

But as soon as I did the day got **100 TIMES BETTER!**

I was on my way over to Maya's house for breakfast, like I do every morning

(her mom cooks like a GODDESS!), and I was going to talk to Maya about...

(1... 2... 3...)

...THE 8th GRADE HALLOWEEN DANCE!!!!

AAAAHHHHHHHH!!!!!

(That was me screaming with excitement!)

I've been waiting for the 8th grade Halloween dance for ages now! (Or for as

long as I've been going to Oakwood Middleschool.)

Now let me just say, I HATE parties.

Almost every time I go to a party, something bad happens to me.

I DON'T KNOW WHY!!!

Sometimes I get locked in the bathroom. Sometimes I spill punch all over myself (or someone else). Sometimes I just can't find the address.

It is my curse.

HOWEVER!

I am really excited to go to this Halloween party because of what it symbolizes: the last *FUN* party you will ever have in middle school.

Everyone always goes over the top for it. Well that's what my older brother, Matt, says anyway.

My brother is a junior in high school and is always telling me about how cool it is!

He's taking honors and advanced placement classes, which basically means he's a smarty pants.

Matt actually wants to be an **author!** Like write books! REAL books! The ones that real people read.

type! type!

I've read some of the stuff he's written— **IT'S RIDONCULOUS!**

Like, just imagine this really funny comedian author (who is actually pretty serious in real life) writes a pre-teens' book about this kid in middle school who has random, hilarious adventures.

THAT'S MY BROTHER!

But anyway, I'm getting off topic.

The point is, Matt has told me all about how AMAZING the Halloween Party is, and that's why I **really** want to go!

The party has a requirement where you have to wear a Halloween costume.

And that's fine by me!

I LOVE dressing up for any occasion! Especially Halloween!

I would always go out trick-or-treating when I was younger. And may I just say, I had some pretty sweet costumes over the years.

Vampire

Alien Hunter

A Legendary Hero

But since none of my friends want to go trick-or-treating with me anymore, I am pretty set on going to this party.

So anyway, after breakfast Maya and I were walking to school, and naturally I had to ask her about what she was going to go as this year.

"I don't know," Maya said. "Maybe a cat again. It's a simple costume."

"What?" I asked. "But that's so **boring!** Don't you want to go as something new and exciting?"

"I'm just not all that into Halloween, Jess," she replied.

"Why not? It's free candy!"

"I don't like walking around the streets at night like a hoodlum," Maya said seriously. "My mom says that's the way you get caught up in gang riots."

I literally hate everything she just said.

"I literally hate everything you just said," I told Maya.

"Look," I continued, "it's an 8th grade party, not a bum-filled street brawl! It'll be fun!"

"I don't know, Jess—"

"*Will is going to be there...*" I interrupted.

Look, I hope none of you folks are interpreting what I said in a weird way. It's not like that. Maya and Will are just besties, but Maya really doesn't have the guts to do **ANYTHING** fun unless Will is gonna be around.

I love the girl to death, but Maya is just a plain old **chicken**.

I actually think it's pretty funny how scared of everything Maya is considering her dream is to become a professional tennis player.

Professional sports usually cause a lot of stress for people, but when it comes to tennis Maya is FEARLESS! And it's the only thing she **ever** talks about (which can get pretty annoying sometimes).

But anyway, let's get back to talking about how Maya is a chicken and doesn't want to wear the stinking Halloween costume.

"What would I even go as?" Maya asked.

"How about a princess?" I replied.

"*Ha, ha,*" Maya said sarcastically, "but seriously?"

"No really," I replied. "you go as a princess, I go as a knight, Will goes as a jester, or a dragon, or—"

"How about a prince?" Maya interrupted.

"Well that's a bit cheesy," I answered, "but, yeah, okay."

When we got to school, Maya and I told Will about our idea.

He seemed pretty excited about our plan, and thought a group costume would be fun...

Our Epic Halloween Costumes

...right until he saw what our costumes actually looked like on us.

How Our Costumes Really Look

That was **not** a pretty picture, my friend!

"We **can't** wear these!!!" Will screamed at me right in the middle of the

Halloween store. "We look **ridiculous!**"

"We don't look *that* ridiculous," I replied.

"Yeah, we kinda **do**," Maya intervened.

"Well, these are the cheapest costumes they have here!" I yelled. "What do you want me to do?"

"How about we just order costumes online," Will replied, while holding up his phone with a picture of the most fantabulous, and reasonably-priced, Halloween costume I've **EVER** seen!

Our New Costumes That Conveniently Look Just Like What We Originally Ordered

"**WOW!** These are perfect!" I screamed. "Order these **IMMEDIATELY!**"

And so he did! The Halloween party is next week, and now that we have our costumes, **NOTHING CAN GO WRONG!!!**

SOMETHING WENT WRONG!!!!

SOMETHING WENT TERRIBLY, TERRIBLY WRONG!!!!

Our costumes just came in and they look AWFUL!

The company that was selling them online messed up our order so instead of

our amazing medieval costumes, we got THIS!

Me in my HORRIBLE
Halloween Costume

LUCHA LIBRE WRESTLERS???!!!!

COMPLETE WITH MASSIVE MUSCLE SUITS AND

MASKS!!!!!!

WHY??!!!!!!

Like, how do you get masked wrestlers confused with medieval knights?!!

We were all **SO** mad!

I mean, we can't wear these!

Not only are the costumes essentially like wearing a balloon, but Maya's costume has huge taco stains on it!

Like, I guess the guys who were packaging the costumes must have been working during lunch because Maya's costume looks like Taco Tuesday gone horribly wrong.

Maya's Costume

Poor Maya burst into tears.

However, because the party is **TOMORROW**, I'm afraid we have no choice but to wear these unusually greasy outfits.

(Though in all honesty, I found it **really** funny to see everybody dressed as gargantuan, masked, torso twisters for Halloween.)

It did take a lot of persuasion and straight up begging to get Will to wear

the costume. But thankfully, Maya, who already promised to wear the outfit,

was able to sway Will to agree.

Will always does what Maya says nowadays, so long as I have Maya on my

team, he'll do whatever I say!

But aside from that one ray of sunlight, this whole thing is a **COMPLETE**

DISASTER!!!

I don't even want to think about what could happen at the actual party.

October 25

So it's party night!

I have a **really** bad feeling about the whole thing.

Like you know when you're planning to go see your cousins and you're super pumped about it but then you remember that your nasty, dog-obsessed aunt is going to be there too, and you're all like, "UGH!!!" Yeah that's basically how I'm feeling about this party tonight.

Oh, my brother Matt is calling me. My mom's forcing him to drive me to the party, so I gotta go! He's been making fun of my hideous costume ALL DAY! So I **really** do not want to get in the car with him right now.

I'm just hoping that this whole night doesn't blow up in my face.

I'll keep you posted.

October 26

Well, last night was a complete **DISASTER!!!**

AAAHHHHH!!!

(That was me screaming.)

Things **literally** could not have gone worse!

So I got to the party, you know, dressed in my nightmare costume. And I got inside the gym, where the dance is being held, and I met up with Will and Maya.

I didn't feel complelety awful about my costume looking stupid cause there was this dude wearing a bright pink dolfin outfit that had the words "I Feel Pretty" plastered on the chest.

(Nevertheless, we still looked pretty dumb in our Halloween costumes.)

HERE COMES THE PARTY!!!!

The party was fine at first. My pals and I ate some food (mostly pizza),

danced for a while, and tried avoiding eye contact from the people who were

probably wondering why in the **world** we would choose to wear something so

insanely **HIDEOUS**.

But after, like, 20 minutes of a somewhat enjoyable party, things

SERIOUSLY started to go downhill!

Okay, so you remember Carol and her janky side-kick, Brenda? Yeah, well,

they were at the party and were being major jerks.

Brenda came as a witch (which was SO on point for her) and Carol came as a

snooty cheerleader (again, excellent choice for her).

I said we should just ignore them...

...HOWEVER!

...Carol and Brenda had other ideas.

I could see the two little nasties chit-chatting with each other, and

whispering things in each other's ears like they were gossiping or something.

After a while I lost sight of the brats and decided to go sit down and eat

some Halloween candy at one of the tables.

But when I sat down, I suddenly heard this huge **POP!**

I quickly shot out of my seat and looked around for what caused the noise.

I couldn't see anything, but then I noticed that my costume started to feel more deflated.

But since my dumb balloon of an outfit was too big for me see anything below my chin, I had to run over to Maya and Will and ask them what was going on with my costume.

"Jess, you have a huge thumb tack sticking out of your butt!" Maya said.

"What?!!" I screamed while trying to see for myself.

And sure enough, she was right.

There was a huge thumb tack jammed right in the butt of my wrestler suit!

"AHHH! Get it out! Get it out!" I demanded.

"Okay," Will said. "I'll get it."

And as soon as he pulled the thing out, all the air came shooting out of my costume like the **biggest fart ever erupted!**

I started to SERIOUSLY panic!

Not only was I wearing the most hideous costume ever, but now I was also wearing the most **DEFLATED** and **FLABBY** costume **ever!**

I didn't want to be remembered as *that kid* whose Halloween costume turned into a saggy potato chip at the party!

So naturally I did what any middle schooler in distress would do: **I fled to the girls' bathroom in shame.**

Maya was yelling something to me, but the party was so loud that I couldn't hear a word she was saying.

But it must have been a warning 'cause as I was running to the bathroom I slammed right into **Dave** (that annoying kid from my wellness class), flopped onto the food table, and landed wrestler-mask-first into the punch bowl.

I was really not having any fun at that point of the night.

When I *finally* made it to the girls' room, I ran into one of the stalls and took off my costume to let it dry. I quickly threw it over the stall door and tried to clean myself off with the cheap toilet paper that was on hand.

I then heard the bathroom door open.

I figured it must have been a random party goer.

Well, all I can say is thank heavens I had leggings on under my costume cause whoever walked into the bathroom just straight up stole my costume from off the door

But I think we all know **who** would be devilish enough to do that: **Carol and**

Brenda!

I bet they even did something to make my costume explode in the first

place!

I was so mad I could **spit!**

I bet those girls put the thumb tack on my seat, knowing I would sit there

and anticipating that I would go to the bathroom so they could steal my

clothes!

I HATE those girls so much!

I mean it's not like I was NAKED or anything, but I didn't want to go walking

around in just my leggings! It was cold outside!

I decided that since I was in school, I would just go raid the lost-and-found box for clothes that I thought would work.

So I snuck out of the bathroom trying to not attract too much attention.

I was able to make it to the lost-and-found box without anyone seeing me, but you know how the lost-and-found box can be: **THEY NEVER HAVE WHAT YOU'RE LOOKING FOR!**

All I wanted was a sweatshirt or sweatpants.

What I got instead was a tutu, a leather jacket, a fedora, and light-up

sneakers that made me look especially stupid.

Well, anything's better than nothing.

After I geared up, I decided to go track down Carol and Brenda to get revenge (or at the very least cause a scene).

But when I got back to the party Brenda and Carol were nowhere to be seen.

I did, however, see Maya and Will searching for me (which was sweet of them).

I would say that it was very sweet of them to want to make sure I was okay, but in their costumes, they kinda looked like two dumplings who were trying to jog in place.

Then from behind me, I heard the sound of pure, vile evil!

"Hey Jess," Carol said sarcastically. "Nice costume. What are you supposed to be anyway? A ballerina, biker, businessman?"

I turned around slowly and glared at the wicked one.

"Give me my costume back, Carol," I demanded. "Now."

"Oh that giant wrestler thing?" Brenda said, walking up behind me. "We threw that thing out. Thought it was garbage."

I wanted to say some awesome, in-your-face-style comeback, but I was actually too mad to say anything. So I just turned around and went over to the DJ and asked him to blast a really loud and obnoxious song.

Then I went out onto the dance floor and started freestyle dancing right in the middle of everyone.

I looked especially ridiculous with my stolen light-up sneakers blinding the other dancers with their sparkly beams.

I think I was dancing so hard that some of the punch, still dripping from my face, was flying into the crowd.

By the time the dance was over and Matt came to pick me up, I looked COMPLETELY DIFFERENT from when I originally went in.

Matt didn't even recognize me when I got in the car.

He took one look at me, hesitated, and then burst out laughing.

"WHAT THE HECK HAPPENED TO YOU IN THERE?" Matt asked me, while still cackling so hard that he started crying.

"I don't wanna talk about it," I replied.

The entire drive home Matt was still laughing!

When he got to a red light, he whipped out his phone and took a picture of me to make his new screen saver!

I was **SO** upset!

The night was an entire flop, and worst of all, **I DIDN'T EVEN GET ANY CANDY!**

WORST HALLOWEEN PARTY EVER!!!

October 31

Okay, so today is **actually** Halloween, and I have **NO** desire to go out

trick-or-treating tonight!

I just wanna hide in my room and watch sitcoms on TV.

That is the only thing that will soothe my soul.

My mom says that I should go out and at least try to have some fun tonight, but I honestly don't think I can endure any more suffering this Halloween.

Besides, even if I did want to go trick-or-treating, Brenda and Carol

deflated and disposed of my costume!

And even if I managed to come up with a new costume, I don't think I could

convince Maya or Will to go out with me, since wearing their Halloween,

ketchup stained, wrestler suits to the party was embarrassing enough!

Making them go out in **PUBLIC** with those things on might be a dealbreaker.

And there is no way I am going trick-or-treating ALONE! (That's pathetic!)

Oh well, maybe next year.

November 4

Happy November everybody!

I am so pumped!

The nightmare Halloween crisis of 8th grade is over and I can finally move on with my life!

And best of all, now I can properly look forward to **CHRISTMAS!!!**

Yes, I know. *What about Thanksgiving?*

Well, I know Thanksgiving is coming up before Christmas, but no one really cares all that much about that holiday.

For my family, Thanksgiving is less of a celebration of all the things we're thankful for and more of an awkward dinner party filled with the scent of despair and a bunch of relatives that don't like each other.

My family is **REALLY** distant!

We're all spread out across the country.

My Aunt Eileen and Uncle Vinney live in Arizona, my Uncle Bobby and Aunt Regina live in Kentucky, and my parents live here in New Jersey.

My grandparents moved out to Pennsylvania a little while ago, too.

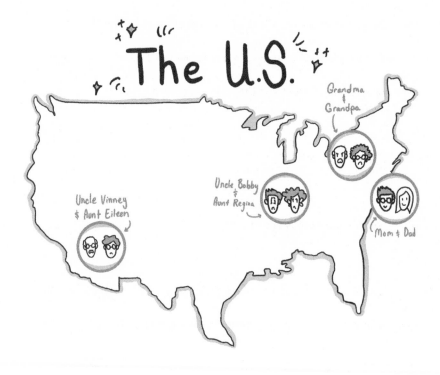

They all started out in Bayonne, New Jersey, but then gradually started moving more and more to the left of the country. My family has never been all that close, and they all have some big beef with my grandpa for some reason.

I don't really know what the big deal is, but whatever the case, Thanksgiving

is **ALWAYS** uncomfortable for **EVERYBODY!**

Last year was an especially huge disaster!

Grandpa and Uncle Bobby started fighting about something, but I was in the

bathroom so I kinda missed the beginning of the argument.

Then Aunt Eileen and Dad started to get into the argument too, and before

the dessert could be served, my relatives were out in my backyard having a

contest to see who could slingshot the most cans off a rock.

Meanwhile, my brother Matt was in the house with my cousin Haylee (who is

the same age as my brother, BTW) raiding the kitchen for the chocolate

cake my mom was baking earlier.

Cousin Haylee

Now I'm the youngest in my family, so no one ever tells me what's going on

with the family feud. I tried asking Matt, but he's always too busy playing

video games with Cousin Haylee to pay attention to me.

Matt and Haylee have been friends ever since she was adopted into the

family when she was two years old. (You know, I wish I was adopted so I

wouldn't have to be related to MATT!!! (Ugh!))

And even though she lives in Arizona with my Aunt Eileen and Uncle Vinney, the two have ALWAYS been video chatting each other and playing video games online together.

I'm pretty sure that my brother and my cousin are the **only** people in my family who actually have a good relationship with each other.

That's why I just wanna get this Thanksgiving over with as soon as possible and move on to the far superior holiday commonly known as:

CHRISTMAS!

(That and 'cause you get presents on Christmas, and all you get on Thanksgiving is dry turkey and the kids' table.)

Let's just hope that nothing goes wrong this year!

Novermber 9

Okay, so I COMPLETELY FORGOT that I had this **HUGE** English paper due today!

I AM COMPLETELY FREAKING OUT!!!

I have no idea what I'm supposed to do. It's like my whole world is crashing down in front of my eyes!

I'm seriously starting to panic!

OH WAIT!

I just remembered that Matt is a hacker! He could just fiddle with my computer and use his nerd powers to stop my teacher from seeing that I didn't do the homework.

My school is very techno focused, and we never actually hand in our homework. We just email it to our teachers. (Matt says my school is just like high school in that way.)

Although I really don't know how all that hacking stuff works, Matt will figure it out for me!

My brother ALWAYS comes through for me!

Sorry, I gotta go talk to Matt. I'll tell you all about how he saved the day for me later!

November 10

MATT SO DID NOT SAVE THE DAY FOR ME!!!

Yesterday was actually a complete disaster!

I ran into my jerk of a brother's bedroom, trying to look as desperate and

pitiful as possible, and THIS IS WHAT HAPPENED!

"Matt, I need you to do me a favor," I screamed in my still-sleeping

brother's ear.

Granted, my first move probably shouldn't have been to give my brother a

heart attack at 6:30 in the morning on a Monday, and then ask him for a

favor.

LOOK, I didn't know he was still asleep!

He's normally getting ready for school around the same time I am, but I think that day he had off from school for some reason. So, yeah, I didn't exactly start off great that morning.

But after Matt realized that I wasn't some masked murderer, and was actually his much worse sister, he calmed down.

"JESS!" he screamed. "What the heck are you doing in here?"

"Matt, there's no time to explain. I just need you to hack my computer so my teacher won't see that I didn't write my paper that's due first thing this morning!"

Matt kinda just stared at me for a second. I think he was still processing what I said.

"It is 6:30 in the morning, and you're telling me that your paper is due at 8:00 when school starts?"

"Yeah, now hurry up and do something techy!" I demanded as I threw my laptop at my brother's face.

"Jess, you have an hour and a half. Why don't **you** just try to write the paper and let **me** sleep," Matt said as he threw his pillow over his head.

"'Cause the paper is about a book that I forgot to read! I wouldn't know what to write!"

"And why do you just expect that *I* would know the book?" he said sarcastically.

"Well, *I DON'T KNOW??!!*" I sarcastically yelled at him. "You were in middle school once, right? Don't all middle schoolers have to read the same junk?"

"You're definitely misconstruing the idea of required reading." (I hate it when Matt uses big words that I don't understand!)

"What's that supposed to mean?" I demanded.

Matt shot up from bed furiously. "Jess, they change the reading requirements for school, like, every few years. So I probably never read any of your books anyway."

"Please, Matt. I need you!"

"Just look at Sparknotes," he said grumpily, pulling the covers over his head.

"No! How about you just help me!"

"Why can't you just do your homework on time and let **me** sleep?"

"UGH! You're useless!" I screamed.

"Love you too, Jess," Matt said sarcastically.

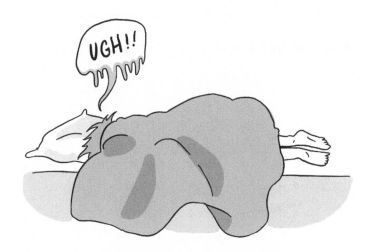

My Useless Brother, Matt

And with that I marched out of my brother's room, with no help, and a

serious problem.

All I've got to say to that is let's just see if I'll be around the next time he needs ME for help with homework. (Yeah, 'cause that'll happen. Dream on, Jess.)

So I got ready for school, got on the bus, and started panic-writing random stuff that may have related to the book I didn't read.

Me Panic-Writing On The Bus

By the time I got to school, it was about 7:58, and I had no choice but to send my teacher what I had before I missed the deadline.

The paper was rough but I thought it was reasonable.

The book I was supposed to read was this gross story about the end of the world or something, but I only managed to read the first page, gave up, and started watching cartoons.

Actually, I think that book is about a dystopia, but since I just assume that all dystopian novels are the same (mostly because they're all equally terrible), I gave it my best guess.

Despite my efforts to write about the book, I don't think my teacher liked my interpretation of the story.

A Paper by Jessica Yermack

I found all the characters super interesting in this book.

They were very cool. I liked the main character the most, because without that

person, there wouldn't be a story, or a happy ending, and the whole world

would probably still have a lot of issues that are pretty bad.

If I had to pick my favorite part of the book, I would say that since I believe

every part of a story should be equally appreciated, morally, I can't in good

conscience make that decision.

This book was indeed very cool. I liked it a lot, and would possibly recommend

it to other people. Thank you for your time.

~~Teh~~ The End.

I ended up getting a D- on that paper and was sent to the principal's office to talk about my lack of respect for my teacher by not doing the assigned homework, or something.

Well, I thought that was a dumb reason to be called into the principal's office. So I told him, "My teacher had it coming by assigning us such a lame book to read."

I recommended that instead we all read superhero comics, 'cause reading that sort of stuff would at least hold **MY** attention. But I don't think my principal liked that idea very much, since he immediately called my mom and dad to come over so they could have a "*talk*" about me.

My parents were super mad at me, and gave me a big lecture on how "All of your teachers have said that you don't pay attention or do any of your classwork." And how "you have to get good grades in school so that you can get into a nice high school like Matt."

UGH!

Applying to high school is SO annoying!

Look, I know, I should've just read the dumb book and done the dumb assignment, but I had things going on in my life, okay? The fifth and final season of this EPIC superhero show was released and I had to binge watch it!

And anyway, I think I did a pretty decent job writing that paper considering I was rushing and was on a bumpy bus ride to school that morning!

But of course, that fact didn't really help stop my parents from grounding me for a week. So that'll be fun.

I'll talk to you when my life stops being a bottomless pit of punishment.

Or not! You people don't control my life!

Unfortunately, my parents do that.

December 19

Okay, so I am kinda **FREAKING OUT!**

(Oh and sorry I haven't written anything in a while, there is a lot of stuff going on right now.)

Christmas is in a few days, and I haven't gotten any presents for anyone! My relatives are coming over tomorrow, and nothing is ready for them!

Matt's having a fashion emergency trying to find something cool to wear when cousin Haylee gets here.

Matt always wants to impress Haylee. That's why he tries to dress *FANCY* whenever she comes to town. He's so dumb, thinking that by dressing like a big shot, Haylee will like him more.

The JERK!

It's SO WEIRD! Especially since they're already best friends as it is! How could Haylee possibly like him any more?

 I can guarantee that that's only going to end badly.

Nevertheless, my brother **always** freaks out when Haylee's coming over. He starts fidgeting with his hair and forcing me to rate his dress shirts on a scale of 1—10 in terms of coolness.

I think he just wants to impress her. BUT WHY DOES IT HAVE TO BE AT **MY** EXPENSE?

High schoolers! Am I right? Always worrying so much about dumb things like that.

What he should be worried about is WHAT THE HECK I SHOULD GET

HIM FOR CHRISTMAS!!!

I am SO not prepared for any of this!

Plus, Maya already made me and Will feel **crazy** guilty by getting us really

fancy three-way friendship bracelets!

I didn't even know they made those!

And Maya took the high road, of course, and was all like, "Oh, you don't have

to get me anything in return. It's what friends do!"

UGH!!!

Maya The Goody-Goody

Of course I'm going to get her something! I have to, now that she got me something! That's how gift-giving works. EVERYBODY KNOWS THAT!

And I bet she knew that when she got us the present! Maya actually wanted me to get her something for Christmas for a change, and this was her diabolical plan to do that!

I KNOW YOUR GAME, MAYA!!!

Will also got me and Maya a gift a few days after. He bought me this new comic book I've wanted FOR EVA!!!! (So now I especially feel like a garbage panda.)

Meanwhile, Will got Maya this really pretty heart-shaped, silver necklace. You know, like the ones where you can stick a tiny photo of someone you like inside.

Will for some reason decided to stick a photo of himself in the necklace, I guess so Maya always remembers that **he's** the one who gave it to her.

Nevertheless, she seemed pretty into it.

Maya's Present From Will

But anyway, let's get back to my family issues.

My Uncle Bobby and Aunt Regina are coming early in the morning tomorrow, since they live closer to us than my Aunt Eileen and Uncle Vinney do. (Quick reminder — Bobby and Regina live in Kentucky and Eileen and Vinney live in Arizona)

My dad and Matt are going to the airport to pick up my Aunt Eileen, Uncle Vinney, and Cousin Haylee when their flight gets in at around 3:40 p.m.

I am really excited to see Haylee, since she's my **ONLY** cousin, but I doubt I'll see her much since she'll probably be hanging out with Matt the whole time.

My mom is FREAKING OUT, though.

She keeps ranting that she doesn't have the guest rooms ready, and the blow-up bed for Haylee has a bunch of holes in it so it won't inflate.

She made me and Matt drive to the store to pick up a new blow-up mattress, but C'MON, like **we** know where to find a blow-up mattress at a moment's notice?

Matt and I drove around a lot. We went to A THOUSAND different department stores but we couldn't find a single mattress.

Mom looked pretty upset when we came home empty handed.

But I did pick up duct tape while we were at one of the stores, so I just used that to patch the holes, and it seemed to work.

*it fixes EVERYTHING!

Matt, however, insisted that Haylee should not have to sleep on that thing

for the six days the family is here, so he volunteered to sleep on the ratty

mattress in the living room while Mom and Dad (who surrendered their bed

to Uncle Bobby and Aunt Regina) took the couch.

I know, I know, that's very sweet of him, but let me tell you right now... **I**

AIN'T GIVING MY BED UP FOR NO ONE!!!

Oh, sorry, I gotta go. My mom's calling me to go help her get the beds out

for my Grandma and Grandpa.

OH! Did I forget to mention? My grandparents are coming over as well!

And considering how well my family gets along, this should be a super fun

Christmas!

(NOT!)

December 21

Well, yesterday was a complete **DISASTER!!!** (Though, I did anticipate

that.) However, I didn't expect things to go awry so quickly this year.

Things started to go wrong the second Uncle Bobby and Aunt Regina arrived.

My Aunt Regina likes to make her family be her slave and do her dirty work

(but don't tell her I said that, please).

Before the woman even walked in the door, she made my mom carry in all her

bags, and trust me, the woman brought a LOT of them!

When my Uncle Bobby walked in, he immediately ran to the back of the house where my dad was barbecuing dinner, probably so he could get away from his wife.

Bobby is always following my dad around to have an excuse to get away from Aunt Regina.

One time, to prove that I was getting something out of my school education, Aunt Regina gave me a math workbook for my birthday, and then **forced me to go through it!**

The woman actually sat there and watched me do the math. And if I made a mistake, she ripped the book out of my hands and started lecturing my mom about how I'm not being educated properly.

Yeah, she's an "interesting" woman to say the least.

Then around 3 o'clock, Matt and dad were about to head out to pick up the others, when Uncle Bobby came out of nowhere and insisted that he "needed" to go with Dad to the airport.

Matt ended up staying at the house, which he wasn't all that happy about. But to be honest, I think Matt ended up avoiding a car ride of pain considering what happened next.

Uncle Vinney and Aunt Eileen arrived, along with Cousin Haylee who decided

to bring her new **BOYFRIEND** with her.

Haylee and her boyfriend,
NICKEY!

I could see the light getting harpooned out of Matt's eyes, and that's when I

realized that this was probably gonna be the WORST family Christmas yet.

Haylee's boyfriend is named Nickey, and he's a senior in high school. He's really tall, and cool, and WAY better looking than Matt! Then again, a **porta potty** is better looking than Matt.

Things were getting seriously awkward. Haylee was introducing her boyfriend to the whole family, while Matt was trying to not scream his head off.

Matt trying not to lose his cool

It is just a guess, but I don't think Matt likes Nickey very much.

It's always been just Haylee and Matt, ever since they met. And now Matt is just a major third wheel, and isn't cool with that **AT ALL!**

Yeah, it sucks being the odd man out. (Now you know how *I* felt all those years you and Haylee ditched *me*, MATT!)

Haylee was sitting with Nickey the whole day, being all lovey-dovey, while Matt was hovering in the corner like the sad sack of potatoes he is.

Every two minutes or so, Matt would start throwing a butt-load of questions at Nickey about his plans for the future and what he wanted to do with his life.

Matt was all, "So **NICKEY**, what exactly do you plan on doing with your life?"

But Nickey readily replied, "Oh, I want to go into robotic design."

"You got any ideas about where you're going to college?"

"I was recently accepted into MIT."

"Do you have any internships?"

"I am planning on getting an internship after I start college, since studies show that's a surefire way to get a job."

And Matt kept on throwing out more and more questions. I don't think the boy even stopped to breathe in between sentences!

Not to mention, Matt seemed **REALLY** upset by how ready Nickey was for those questions.

My pathetic brother ended up sitting next to them on the couch and pouting in silence for, like, twenty minutes after he finished his ~~interrogation~~ chat with Nickey.

So, so sad.

I, however, have more self-respect and decided to hang out with Uncle Vinney (who always liked me best).

We ended up playing cards until my grandparents arrived.

When they got here, things were calm for about an hour before fighting broke out.

My grandma started commenting on how my mom and Aunt Eileen were making salad, setting the table, and just about everything in general.

The ladies started to get snippy with each other, which turned into bickering, and then arguing.

My grandpa challenged my Uncle Vinney to an arm wrestling competition, which quickly escalated into a wrestling match, and soon turned into a cage fight in our living room.

My Aunt Regina started to yell at Matt about how he should rub her sore feet, because "back in her day" she would have been "happy" to rub her aunt's nasty feet.

But Matt definitely did not want to do that.

Then, to make matters worse, Nickey started to lecture Matt about how he should respect his elders and do what Aunt Regina said.

That statement didn't go over well and then transformed into a three-way argument between Matt, Nickey, and Aunt Regina. Then Cousin Haylee tried to break up the fight which only ended with her arguing, too.

My Uncle Bobby didn't seem too interested in arguing with anyone so he simply laid down on the living room floor, drinking soda. That is, until Dad started yelling at him to get off the ground.

Meanwhile, I waited for dinner.

Later that night when things calmed down, because we didn't know **NICKEY**

would be coming for a visit, Matt ended up having to **SHARE HIS**

MATTRESS WITH HIM!!!

HA!

Here's the schedule for where everyone is sleeping in my house...

We have two guest rooms:

- Grandma and Grandpa were in one.

- Uncle Vinney and Aunt Eileen were in the other.

- Aunt Regina and Uncle Bobby got my parents' room.

- Haylee got Matt's room.

- Matt and Nickey were sharing the busted mattress in the living room.

- Mom and Dad are crashing on the living room couch.

- And I am staying in my room!

House Plan:

Cousin Haylee

me

Grandma & Grandpa

Aunt Regina & Uncle Bobby

blah, blah, blah, blah

stairs

Kitchen

Mom, Dad, Matt & Nickey

Uncle Vinney & Aunt Eileen

Matt was REALLY unhappy about having to share a bed with Nickey, aka *the boyfriend.*

Today, Matt told me all about how last night Nickey was lying all over him, crowding the whole bed, and actually put Matt in a **headlock** while asleep!

11:30 p.m.

2:00 a.m.

4:50 a.m.

I am literally STILL laughing at that!

And we have five more days with these nut baskets!

Man, Christmas is going to be fun!

December 26

WOW!

Just wow.

Christmas was certainly interesting.

My relatives left a few minutes ago, and we couldn't be happier that they're

gone.

I don't even know how to begin telling you this story, but I think I should

just start by saying this: in all my life, I have never gotten Christmas

presents that were as unbelievably TERRIBLE as they were this year!

This year I got a science workbook from my Aunt Regina, which she was prepared to ~~force~~ watch me complete, but my mom insisted that I would use it another time.

Some kids get scratchy sweaters and socks for Christmas... I get **textbooks.**

Matt and Haylee both got these really pricey calculators from Regina and Bobby, while Nickey the newbie got nada.

Aunt Eileen and Uncle Vinney gave me the best present that a girl could ask for: a check!

But it was kind of a letdown when I saw that it was only for 10 dollars. They gave Matt a check, too, but since Haylee's their daughter she got these really cool paint-based graffiti pens! They were awesome!

Of course, Aunt Regina said that getting a child graffiti pens will turn them into a hoodlum and street ruffian, but no one cared.

Grandma and Grandpa gave us kids coloring books, like we were four years old. But they **ONLY** gave us the coloring books, no crayons or anything.

Grandpa was all like, "What? Do I look like I'm made of money to you? You got the coloring book. Be grateful kid."

Mom and Dad gave me a few new video games, and Matt got this nifty typewriter that he's been wanting since he was two.

My parents gave Haylee another check, and all my aunts and uncles got pastry baskets.

Actually, all my relatives gave each other pastry baskets. I don't know what the deal with that is. I think it's cause baked goods are the only thing they can all agree are **AMAZING!!!**

Haylee gave me this book on blogging and a how-to guide to becoming internet famous, which was nice.

She gave my brother this exclusive, insanely hard-to-come-by, limited-edition action figure from some TV show made in the 80's they like where grown men run around in tights and look like mutant cats for whatever reason.

I thought Matt was going to pee his pants. He gave Haylee a really big hug and started caressing the toy's box like a creepy mad-scientist.

Matt then gave Haylee this really pretty charm bracelet that had a bunch of cheesy charms that related to all the things they've done together whenever we have family visits.

Haylee's Charm bracelet

They would always sneak out of the house to go do things together when the

family was busy screaming at each other. I mean, I guess that's a sweet

sentiment. However, I prefer cash.

Meanwhile, all Matt gave **me** was a red hat that had the word "HAT" written

on it in big bold letters for no reason whatsoever.

My brother spared no expense with that present.

Gift-giving didn't involve all that much fighting, but that moment of peace

didn't last long.

Two hours later, after we were all dressed for church, Nickey kept trying to get Haylee to stand under the mistletoe with him, but Matt kept pulling her away to "talk to her."

Matt is such a wuss when he knows he's being replaced by someone else.

Just let it go man! You're not her only friend anymore. MOVE ON WITH YOUR LIFE!

But, of course, Matt saw Nickey as a **major** threat to his friendship with Haylee and asked me to help break them up.

Normally I'd jump at the chance to mess with people, but on Christmas all I wanted to do was play video games. But Matt was persuasive and bribed me with his check from Uncle Vinney and Aunt Eileen, and he swore that he'd clean my room for the next month. So I agreed.

The plan was simple:

1. I distract Nickey and tell him all the terrible things about Haylee, like that she kicks you in your sleep or something. You know, stuff that would make him want to break up with her.

2. Matt distracts Haylee and tries to prove to her that Nickey is a horrible person who she should punch in the face (even though **I** actually like Nickey).

3. Successfully complete our mission and get them to break up, we high five in slow motion, go get milkshakes, roll end credits.

Of course that didn't happen.

What **did** happen was WAY less successful.

I managed to get Nickey to hang out with me for about a half an hour.

I made him watch a bunch of lame chick-flicks with me (because

EVERYONE hates those movies). Then I had him braid my hair, rub my

feet, and help me finish an 800 piece puzzel.

Things were going great with distracting him. The problem was that I

completely forgot about the part where I was supposed to convince him to

break up with Haylee.

Meanwhile, things with Matt and Haylee were failing pretty badly. I don't

know all the details, but I'm pretty sure it ended in a long ~~argument~~

discussion where Haylee explained to Matt that he wasn't the boss of her

and didn't get to decide who she could date.

But that's just a guess since I saw Matt go racing out of the house ten minutes later to go kick all the flowers in our garden.

Matt Beating Up Our Flowers

But that wasn't the only bad part of the day.

My mom was planning on cooking us a big family-sized turkey for dinner, and everyone was really looking forward to it (especially me, who was sitting in the kitchen trying to steal any food I could get my hands on).

And I don't know why my mom decided to walk out of the kitchen, but it sure was a bad idea.

One minute things were fine and the next...

BOOM!

The turkey completely EXPLODED in the oven! There were turkey guts

EVERYWHERE!

My mom screamed and ran into the kitchen, alongside my Aunt Regina, Grandma, Dad, and Uncle Vinney, to find the oven utterly ruined.

And the explosion must have startled my Aunt Eileen, cause she was holding an opened jar of canned pumpkin, which she suddenly dropped on the floor, causing all the pumpkin to fling out of the can, hitting everyone in the kitchen, and even managed to make its way onto the ceiling!

The only food we had prepared to eat that night besides the ruined turkey was the salad, which was now completely covered in pumpkin!

But more importantly...

...now I was COMPLETELY COVERED IN PUMPKIN!!!

The Great Yermack Family Pumpkin Disaster

So basically, half of us were covered in orange OOZE, we had no food, and we were all REALLY hungry.

My aunts and uncles helped my parents clean up the mess while Haylee ordered Chinese food.

By the time Haylee left to grab the food, the kitchen was almost clean.

We ended up speed-eating dinner so we could make it to church on time for Mass.

The ride over to church wasn't that bad. We originally were all going to drive over to Mass together in ONE CAR (to "bond" as a family or something), but Matt decided to take his car and go by himself.

Naturally, I hopped into his car right before he pulled out so I didn't have to ride with the rest of my family.

What? Look, you've seen my relatives all together! They're raving, screaming lunatics when they're just in my house, so imagine what they're like crammed in my parents' minivan!

There was **NO WAY** I was going to sit through that! (Plus, Matt's car has a

better radio.)

We did end up making it there on time, but some of us still had pumpkin on

our clothes.

But like everything else this Christmas, church ended up being a **COMPLETE**

DISASTER!!!

For starters, I had to go to the bathroom a few minutes after Mass started.

So I went into the girls' room, and as I was leaving, I found that the door

wouldn't open!

The door handle was stuck, so I was trapped in there.

I tried body slamming the door a few times, to no avail.

I then tried texting my mom to come save me, but I forgot that she always keeps her phone on silent at church.

I tried for my dad, who didn't pick up the phone.

My last resort was Matt, who was still not in the best mood.

Not my first choice, but thankfully he picked up the phone and came to my rescue!

Well he tried to come to save me, but the dumb butt-clown couldn't find the bathrooms, so I had to try and be his navigation device while on the phone!

When he finally found me, Matt tried to jiggle the handle, which didn't

budge. So then he tried picking the lock... by slamming it with a random

candle he found somewhere.

By some miracle, Matt managed to get me out of my poop-scented prison

just in time to receive Communion.

We went up to the altar with the rest of the church and made our way back to our seats.

But as we were shuffling back down the row to our mom and dad, Matt saw Haylee and Nickey holding hands and being all romantic-like.

And in that brief moment of internal screaming, Matt stopped paying attention to where he was going and accidentally ran into an old man's legs and fell headfirst into the knee rest, which certainly distracted everyone from whatever the priest was saying.

And wouldn't you know it, that old man ended up being none other than...

... MR. GRIBBINS!!!

Matt Falling Over Mr. Gribbins

That poor man can't catch a break!

Dad had to pull Matt off our traumatized neighbor, who was less injured

than **REALLY** surprised.

Matt was fine too, but I do think his pride was bruised pretty badly after publicly humiliating himself in front of not only our whole family but also the whole town.

Yeah, Christmas was kind of a bust, but on the bright side, at least we all have the new year to look forward to!

I have a feeling that it's going to be a **GREAT NEW YEAR!**

And I also have a feeling that you're going to be hearing about it.

You wanna know why?

Cause one of my other Christmas presents my mom got me was ANOTHER **DIARY!!!!**

UGH!!!

So TOTALLY **LAME!!!**

~~Teh~~ The End

(for now...)

Dear random people I may have made sutle references to in this book,

Please don't be mad that I (may or may not have) talked about you in

my story. Me mentioning you (in this soon-to-be New York Times

Best-Seller) is a term of endearment. It means I like you and wanted to

quote your awesomeness for my readers to enjoy! (Though I can not

confirm nor deny that I in any way did such a thing.)

Plus, I looked up copyright infringement laws, and I'm pretty sure I

didn't write anything that could land me in jail.

And even if I did: COME ON, DUDE! I'm just a teenager who doesn't

even have a pension!

Take a chill pill, ya hippies!

—Alex M.

Special Thanks To

Ms. Williamson

Meet ME!!!

(The Author and Illustrator)

Well, I think we can all agree that this Alex girl is pretty much a GENIUS!!!

So wise, so ahead of her time.

She currently lives in the pit of despair commonly known as New Jersey.

She has been writing and drawing for many years now, and is REALLY hoping

that you like her book so she can publish more of her work, become super

famous, and live happily ever after!!!

She is also currently speaking in the third person.

(That's writer lingo, BTW!)

Made in the USA
Coppell, TX
03 September 2020

36606773R00146